# Wide-Awake!

ORIGINAL TITLE:

Polar Bolero, A Bedtime Dance

# Wide-Awake!

ORIGINAL TITLE:
Polar Bolero, A Bedtime Dance

## Debi Gliori

SCHOLASTIC INC.

New York  Toronto  London  Auckland  Sydney
Mexico City  New Delhi  Hong Kong  Buenos Aires

# For Jo, my mum,
# with all my love

Original title: *Polar Bolero, A Bedtime Dance*

ISBN 0-439-42561-1

12 11 10 9 8 7 6 5 4 3 2                    7 8 9 0/0

Printed in the U.S.A.                    24

First Scholastic printing, November 2002

The illustrations in this book were done in watercolor
on Winsor & Newton acid-free watercolor paper.
The display type was set in Berliner.
The text type was set in Souvenir.

The sun has gone down . . .

and the moon's flying high,
trailing fat clouds across the night sky.

But I'm too hot to sleep.

So I toss off the sheet, wriggle toes into slippers,

and creep. . . .

I'm a thing

that goes BUMP

in the night.

out the door,

past the gate,

through the deep summer grasses at the edge of the lawn . . .

to the place where the

wide-awake meet.

There's music and laughter
drifting up from the trees

as we Polar Bolero
with the owls and the bees.

Over oceans and mountains, across rivers and streams . . .

the Polar Bolero makes
you DANCE in your dreams.

So back
we go home
to where
someone cares,
falling into
our pillows,
gently hugging
our bears.

In the dark comes
*my* someone. . . .
She goes HUG
in the night,

kisses me softly,

and whispers, "Sleep tight."